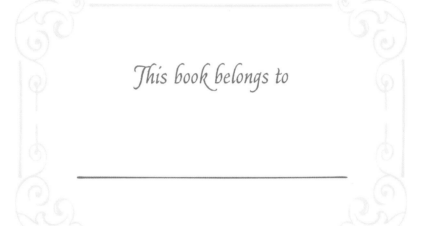

This book belongs to

Asleep on the Hay

A DUST BOWL CHRISTMAS

WRITTEN AND ILLUSTRATED BY

BEN SOWARDS

ENSIGN
PEAK

For my family

Acknowledgments:
Thanks to Connie Sowards and Chris Schoebinger
for their genius and faith during this project.

Interior texture and design elements by Shutterstock.com, © Milanares, © Elena Kalistratova, © ksana-gribakina, © Art'nLera

Text and illustrations © 2015 Ben Sowards

Visit us at EnsignPeakPublishing.com

Library of Congress Cataloging-in-Publication Data

Sowards, Ben, author.
Asleep on the hay : a Dust Bowl Christmas / Ben Sowards.
pages cm
Summary: "Paul's family has struggled to make ends meet during the devastating dust storms of the Midwest. When a family arrives in need, Paul must choose between helping the family or saving his beloved calf. A Christmas miracle helps him learn the true meaning of the season"—Provided by publisher.
ISBN 978-1-62972-067-8 (hardbound : alk. paper)
[1. Families—Fiction. 2. Dust Bowl Era, 1931–1939—Fiction. 3. Depressions—1929—Fiction 4. Christmas—Fiction. 5. Oklahoma—History—20th century—Fiction.] I. Title.
PZ7.1.S69As 2015
[Fic]—dc23   2015003011

Printed in the United States of America by Publishers Printing
10 9 8 7 6 5 4 3 2 1

Peace I leave with you, my peace I give unto you:
not as the world giveth, give I unto you. Let not your
heart be troubled, neither let it be afraid.

JOHN 14:27

P aul pushed through the wind as he led his calf, Ellie, to the safety of the barn and slid the heavy door shut. Inside, they were protected from the violent storm, but dust still hung thick around them. Paul knew one thing for certain—no matter how much he drank or spit, the taste of dust would always be in his mouth.

He spat again and wiped the dust from his calf's eyes and nose. Just before Ellie was born, black dust clouds had destroyed Paul's family's farm, suffocated their crops and livestock, and chased his parents west in search of work. This Christmas it would be just him, his grandfather, and Ellie. With her, maybe Christmas wouldn't be so lonely.

W hen the dust storm passed, Grandfather scraped the last of the beans from an old pot into two small bowls. Paul's stomach growled as his grandfather's rough voice said grace. "And please bless us to truly appreciate the gift of thy Son this Christmas." As his grandfather finished, Paul heard a knocking at the door. Could his parents have returned for Christmas? Paul jumped off the chair, ran to the door, and pulled it open.

Two pairs of unfamiliar eyes met his. A woman held a bundled baby in her arms. The baby cried and then coughed. The man at the door explained that their truck had broken down during the storm. Without hesitating, Grandfather invited the strangers to stay and eat.

Paul watched in disbelief as Grandfather scooped out half of each bowl into two empty ones. Paul ate his beans one at a time. As he watched his grandfather and the man leave to check on the truck, his stomach felt as empty as his bowl.

He left to find Ellie. He wanted to be far away from the noise of the crying baby. He'd rather play a game of "chase the rooster" with Ellie anyway.

When Paul returned to the house, his grandfather and the couple were waiting for him. No one moved. The baby fussed and coughed.

"Paul," his grandfather began in a voice that was unusually soft and low, "these good folks need to get their little one to a doctor. But to do that they need their truck fixed. That costs money and, well, they don't have enough.... Paul, I am very sorry, but we really only have one thing left we can sell to help."

Paul watched his grandfather's lips, but the words were jumbled and far away. His head pounded and his lip quivered. Sensing his pain, the young mother stepped close and pressed a small box into Paul's hands. He avoided her gaze by staring at the words printed on one side of the box. She gently whispered in his ear before he twisted away and ran for the barn.

When Paul reached Ellie, he threw the box down. It shattered, sending its contents tumbling across the floor. He threw his arms around his calf's neck. He would not sell Ellie. Not to fix a truck! Not for these strangers! They would have to sell *him* first.

Still, the words printed on the box would not leave his mind. Paul knew it was a Bible verse. His grandfather had read it to him before. "Peace I give unto you. . . . Let not your heart be troubled, neither let it be afraid."

Ellie sighed. Like the calm after the dust storm, Paul's rage was replaced by stillness. Tears traced clean trails on his cheeks. As he wiped his eyes, he noticed a colorful piece of wood half-hidden beneath the hay. Ellie nudged Paul with her wet nose. He stretched to pick it up.

It was a wooden puzzle piece. Paul looked around and saw many more pieces that had scattered from the broken box. He began to collect the pieces and examine them carefully, one by one. As he fit the pieces together, he began to see part of a picture. He searched to find and place the remaining wooden shapes until the darkness grew too thick.

He had all but the final piece. Paul knew where Grandfather kept the lantern and how to light it, but first, he decided to rest his burning eyes for just a minute or two. He curled up next to Ellie, who was already asleep on the hay.

Paul woke to find himself lying on perfectly flat stones in a building much larger and cleaner than the barn. Standing up quickly, he almost tripped on the long, scratchy shirt he was wearing. A goblet ricocheted across the floor, and Paul pressed himself deeper into the shadows, peeking around a corner.

A loud and powerful voice echoed through the great hall. "Gone? How dare those wise men leave without telling me where to find this baby king!" His hands clenched. "Go to Bethlehem! Find the baby. I want him dead!" He flipped a platter from a servant's hand. "I am the only king! I am Herod the Great!"

Paul didn't know how he had arrived there, but with a jolt he realized King Herod was talking about killing the baby Jesus. Paul knew he had to find Mary and Joseph and warn them. He quickly slipped through the shadows and out of the palace.

Paul struggled to find his way to Bethlehem, and his task only became more difficult after that. The few people who were willing to talk to him knew nothing of a baby named Jesus. Frustrated and exhausted, he sat down for the first time all day. As he took a deep breath, he heard the familiar sound of a calf's call. His heart skipped a beat. He squinted into the setting sun.

He felt guilty for allowing himself to be distracted, but Paul found himself approaching the calling calf as it drank from a low basin. He scratched her head for a moment, then sat down and looked at the water. He suddenly realized how thirsty he was. Even in this faraway place, the taste of dust was in his mouth.

Are you truly so thirsty, boy?" said a voice close behind him.

Startled, Paul turned and saw an outstretched arm. He let the man pull him to his feet.

"Come with me," the man said. "You feel cold. Are you lost? Come and have a bite to eat."

Paul's stomach growled, but he said, "No. I have to find the baby named Jesus. If King Herod's soldiers find him, they will kill him. I've been searching all day. There's no time left. The soldiers are on their way!"

He repeated the urgency of his mission as the man led him through a nearby doorway. Looking in past the animals, he saw a beautiful woman resting on the hay. Her kind eyes fixed on him curiously.

"This boy has traveled a long distance to bring us an important message, Mary," the man said. "I have invited him to share our food."

Mary leaned over a small manger and picked up a tiny bundle. She smiled and approached Paul, who stared in awe.

Sensing his disbelief, the young mother pressed the small bundle into Paul's arms. His eyes focused on the sleeping infant, but he heard Mary gently whisper in his ear, "Peace I give unto you. . . . Let not your heart be troubled, neither let it be afraid."

As the weight of the sleeping baby rested against his chest, Paul felt light. He was at peace.

Ellie's tongue was like sandpaper against his cheek, and the straw-strewn floor stretched sideways before him. Dust floated in a beam of sunlight that split the darkness. It drew a line across the floor that led his eye to a glimmer of light by the feeding trough. As his fingers closed around the puzzle's final piece, he recognized the sleeping face of the tiny baby Jesus.

He looked down at the completed puzzle and smiled. He took the rope from its hook and knelt down next to Ellie. She let him loop it around her neck as she always did. Her eyelashes tickled his cheeks as if she were trying to wipe away his tears.

This gift would require every bit of strength he had. His heart began to pound, and he repeated the whispered words again and again. "Peace I give unto you. . . . Let not your heart be troubled, neither let it be afraid."

A baby's cry floated across the still morning air and lifted him to his feet.

Paul gripped the rope firmly, gave a little tug, and stepped out of the darkness and into the light.